P9-BZQ-467

THE BOXCAR CHILDREN®

SURPRISE ISLAND

Time to Read™

Time to Read™ is an early reader program designed to guide children to literacy success regardless of age or grade level. The program's three levels correspond to stages of reading readiness, making book selection straightforward, and assuring that when it's time for a child to read, the right book is waiting.

— Level 1 —	Beginning to Read	• Large, simple type	• Word repetition
		• Basic vocabulary	• Strong illustration support

— Level 2 —	Reading with Help	• Short sentences	• Simple dialogue
		• Engaging stories	• Illustration support

— Level 3 —	Reading Independently	• Longer sentences	• Short paragraphs
		• Harder words	• Increased story complexity

Library of Congress Cataloging-in-Publication data is on file with the publisher.

Copyright © 2018 by Albert Whitman & Company
Hardcover edition first published in the United States of America
in 2018 by Albert Whitman & Company
Paperback edition first published in the United States of America
in 2019 by Albert Whitman & Company
ISBN 978-0-8075-7679-3

All rights reserved. No part of this book may be reproduced or transmitted in any
form or by any means, electronic or mechanical, including photocopying,
recording, or by any information storage and retrieval system,
without permission in writing from the publisher.

THE BOXCAR CHILDREN® is a registered
trademark of Albert Whitman & Company.

Printed in China
10 9 8 7 6 5 4 3 2 1 WKT 22 21 20 19 18

Interior art by Shane Clester

Visit the Boxcar Children online at www.boxcarchildren.com.
For more information about Albert Whitman & Company,
visit our website at www.albertwhitman.com.

100 Years of Albert Whitman & Company
Celebrate with us in 2019!

THE BOXCAR CHILDREN®

SURPRISE ISLAND

Based on the movie *Surprise Island*
Based on the book by Gertrude Chandler Warner

Albert Whitman & Company
Chicago, Illinois

"Today is the best!"
said Benny Alden.
School was over.
It was finally summer.
"I wonder what Grandfather
has planned," said Henry.
"He said he had a surprise."

Benny could not wait to find out.
"Race you!" he called,
running ahead.
Henry, Jessie, and Violet
couldn't wait either.
They ran to catch up.

At home, Grandfather was
in the garden.
The children had not always
lived with Grandfather.
They had once lived in a boxcar.
That was where they found
their dog, Watch.
Living in a boxcar had been
a big adventure.
The Aldens loved adventures.

The children gathered around
Grandfather.

"Tell us!" Benny said.

"It's summer and we all want to
know," said Jessie.

Grandfather smiled.

He waited for the children
to sit.

Then he told them the surprise.

"Our family has an island,"
he said.
"I stayed there in the summer
when I was a boy.
Now you can too! We can
go see it this afternoon."

The children had many questions.

"Will we be alone?" asked Henry.

Grandfather shook his head.

"Captain Daniel lives there.

He takes care of the island."

"What will we do?" asked Violet.

"I used to explore, swim,

and fish," said Grandfather.

"Can Watch come?" asked Benny.

"Of course!" Grandfather said.

Jessie made a list of things
to bring.
They all packed and got
into the car.
A new adventure!

At the dock, a man was waiting.
"Is that a pirate?" asked Benny.
Grandfather laughed.
"That is Captain Daniel,"
he said. "He's a fisherman."

"All aboard," Captain Daniel
called.
Soon the boat was on its way.

The boat skimmed
across the water.
Before long, Henry pointed.
"There it is!" he said. "Our very
own island!"

Benny started to wave.

"What are you doing, Benny?"
Jessie asked.

"I'm saying hello to the island,"
he said.

Everyone laughed.

They all waved to the island.

There was a small cottage on shore. "Is that where we will stay?" asked Violet.

"That is Captain Daniel's house," said Grandfather. "You get to stay somewhere special." He led the children up the hill.

At the top was a big red barn.
Benny's eyes got big. "We get
to live in there?" he asked.
Grandfather nodded.
The children rushed inside.

Benny found a horse stall.

"We'll sleep in here!" he said.

Jessie found a stove.

"We can cook here!" she said.

Violet went upstairs.

"Let's make crafts up here!"
she said.

"Well, do you like it?" asked
Grandfather. "Do you want
to stay?"

"We love it," said Benny.
The children agreed.
They would stay for the summer.
All by themselves!

At the dock, the children
hugged Grandfather.

"We'll miss you," said Violet.

"Don't worry," he said. "I'll visit.
Benny's birthday is coming up,
after all."

Grandfather got on the boat
and left with Captain Daniel.

The children went to the barn.

They had a lot to do!

Violet and Benny unpacked.

Henry went to get water.

Jessie made supper.

It was like living in the boxcar!

In the morning a young man
came up the path.

"Hello," he said. "I'm Joe. I
work for Captain Daniel."

Joe showed them a
garden they could
use for food.

Then he said,
"If you need
anything else,
just let me
know."

Violet watched as Joe
walked away.
She knew him from someplace.
But where?

The afternoon was warm
and sunny.
Benny was excited to explore.
"Let's dig for treasure!" he said.

The children walked to the beach.
A spurt of water came up from
the sand.
"What was that?" asked Violet.
There was another spurt.
"Clams!" said Henry.
The children started to dig.
Soon they had a whole
bucket of clams!

Down the beach, the children
found another surprise. A raft!
Henry and Jessie swam out to it.
The water was cold.
But the raft was warm.
Henry lay in the sun.
"This is the best," he said.

But Benny did not think so.
He stayed on the beach
with Violet.
"I like warm water," he said.
Benny sat in the sand and
picked at some seaweed.

"What do you have there?"
a voice called.
Benny looked.
It was Joe.

"Watch this," said Joe. "It spreads
out big when it gets wet."
Joe set the seaweed in the water.
Then he caught it on a piece
of paper.
"It's beautiful," said Violet.
Benny smiled.
The beach wasn't so bad
with Joe around.

After swimming, Jessie found
a pretty shell.
Benny showed Jessie his
seaweed and a purple flower.
"That gives me an idea," said
Henry. "Let's make a museum!"
"Great idea!" said Violet.

The children walked
up and down the beach.
They found all kinds
of neat things to put
in their museum.

That night Jessie cooked the clams for supper.
Then they started on their museum.

Joe came over with a stack of books. He helped the children find the names of their objects.

"My flower!" said Benny.
"It's a beach pea!"
"That's right," said Joe.
He turned to Jessie, "And that
is a slipper shell."
Joe seemed to know something
about all the objects they had
found.

The next morning it
rained and rained.
"No exploring today," said Jessie.
She made lunch with vegetables
from the garden.

In the afternoon, the children
worked on their museum.
Violet pressed flowers.
Henry cut out paper birds.
Jessie sorted shells.
"I don't mind the rain at all!"
said Benny.

Days passed.

The museum grew.

Then one day Violet said,

"Let's go all the way to the end of the island!"

"Yeah!" Benny said.

"Maybe there's treasure there!"

The children walked and walked.

Finally, Benny stopped.

"Look," he said. "A mountain!"

It was actually a big pile of clamshells.

"I wonder how it got here,"
said Violet.

"It's a mystery," said Jessie.

The children came to the end
of the island.
But Benny still ran ahead.
"Over here!" he said. "A cave!"
Benny crawled into a dark hole.
Henry, Jessie, Violet, and
Watch followed.
As they went, the hole got
bigger and bigger.
"Wow," said Jessie. "It's like
a little room."

"I think Watch found something!"
said Henry.

He picked up a sharp stone
Watch had dug up.

"It looks like an old tool,"
said Jessie. "I wonder where it
came from."

"Another mystery!" said Benny.

Suddenly, Watch barked from
the front of the cave.

The children turned around.

Water was coming in!

"Let's get out of here!"
said Henry.

The children crawled back
through the hole.
Water rose around them.
"A big wave is coming!"
said Henry. "Hold on!"
Jessie grabbed onto Benny
as the wave passed.

Then she pulled him onto
the rocks.

"That was close," Benny said.
"Good thing we have such
a good watchdog."

Henry nodded. "Let's go dry off."

Along the path, the children
met Joe.
He brought them to the cottage
to warm up.
Henry showed Joe the rock tool.
"This is very old," said Joe.
"Can you take me to where you
found it?"

When it was safe, the children
went back to the cave.
Joe brought along a brush and
a camera.
He showed them how to dig
carefully.

"I found something!" said Jessie.

"Me too!" said Violet.

They held up two small objects.

"Is it treasure?" asked Benny.

"Not treasure," said Joe. "Parts of a bowl! I think people lived on this island long ago."

"That explains my tool," said Henry.

"And the clamshell mountain!" said Benny.

"You helped us solve our mystery, Joe!" said Jessie. "What a neat surprise!"

But an even bigger surprise
was yet to come.

As days passed, the children
tried many new things.
Joe taught Violet how
to play the violin.
Henry taught Benny how to fish.

Jessie learned how to sail.
The summer was full of
adventures.
Just like they had hoped.

Then it was Benny's birthday.
Time for Grandfather to visit!
Joe and Violet played Benny
a birthday song.
When they were done, there
was a knock on the door.
"Grandfather!" said Benny.
But another man walked in.

The man was looking for Joe.
"This is Mr. Browning,"
Joe explained. "My boss."
"Boss?" asked Henry. "I thought
you worked for Captain Daniel."
Joe told them a secret.
He used to work at a museum!
"That's how you knew so much
about our museum!" said Henry.
"And about
digging
stuff up!"
said
Benny.

"Why did you leave the museum?"
asked Violet.

"I got hurt," Joe said.
"I needed to rest."

"But why did you come here?"
Jessie asked.

"Well, I came here as a boy,"
said Joe. "You see, this is my
island too. I'm your cousin!"

Violet's eyes got big.

"That's it!" she said. "I remember
now. I saw you in Grandfather's
pictures!"

"Why didn't you tell us, Joe?"
Jessie asked.

Joe said he and Grandfather
did not always get along.
He was afraid Grandfather
would be mad he was
on the island.
"No way!" said Benny.
"You're the best!"
They would soon find out
what Grandfather thought.

Grandfather arrived that
afternoon.

The children met him at the dock.

"I have a surprise for you,"
he told Benny. Grandfather
pulled out a present.
"No, I have a surprise
for you!" said
Benny.

Benny led Grandfather up the hill.
When they got to the barn,
Joe walked out.

"Joe!" said Grandfather. "I'm
so happy to see you!"
Joe smiled. "I'm glad I came back."

At dinner, the children told
Grandfather everything.
"It sounds like you and
Joe have had quite the summer,"
said Grandfather.
"We have!" said Benny. "It's too
bad we will have to leave soon."

Grandfather and Joe talked quietly.
They made a decision.
Joe was going to live with them!
"I can't wait to show you the
boxcar, Joe!" said Benny.

Soon summer was over.

It was time to go home.

The children sat on the beach one last time.

Violet said, "This place was full of surprises."

That gave Jessie an idea.

"That's what we should call it," she said. "Surprise Island!"

Benny sighed. "I never did find any treasure."

"No?" asked Joe. "I know I did. My family!"

The children packed their things.
"Good-bye, barn," said Jessie.
"See you next summer."

They all got on Captain
Daniel's boat.
On the way home,
Benny looked back.
He waved.
Everyone smiled.
They all waved
good-bye to
Surprise Island.

Keep reading with the Boxcar Children!

Henry, Jessie, Violet, and Benny are orphans. They need to find a place where they can live together as a family. So when they find a boxcar in the woods, they decide to call it home—and become the Boxcar Children. Adapted from the beloved chapter book, this new early reader allows kids to begin reading with the story that started it all.

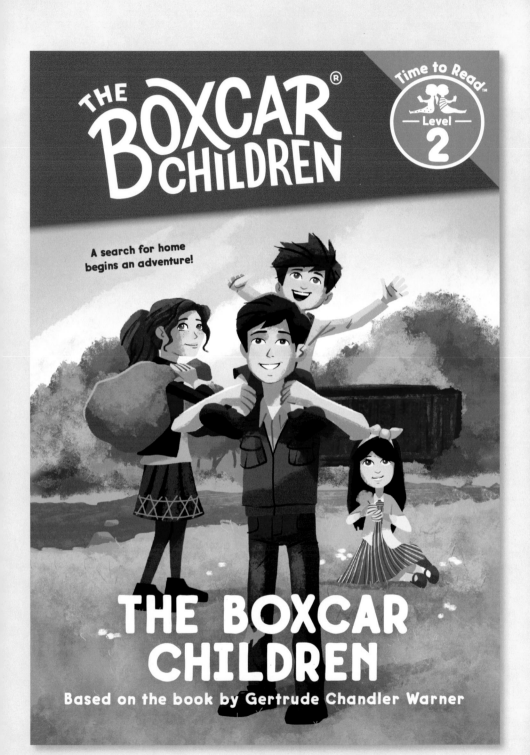

Time to Read™
Level 2

THE BOXCAR® CHILDREN

A search for home begins an adventure!

THE BOXCAR CHILDREN

Based on the book by Gertrude Chandler Warner

GERTRUDE CHANDLER WARNER discovered when she was teaching that many readers who like an exciting story could find no books that were both easy and fun to read. She decided to try to meet this need, and her first book, *The Boxcar Children*, quickly proved she had succeeded.

Miss Warner drew on her own experiences to write the mystery. As a child she spent hours watching trains go by on the tracks opposite her family home. She often dreamed about what it would be like to set up housekeeping in a caboose or freight car—the situation the Alden children find themselves in.

While the mystery element is central to each of Miss Warner's books, she never thought of them as strictly juvenile mysteries. She liked to stress the Aldens' independence and resourcefulness and their solid New England devotion to using up and making do. The Aldens go about most of their adventures with as little adult supervision as possible— something else that delights young readers.

Miss Warner lived in Putnam, Connecticut, until her death in 1979. During her lifetime, she received hundreds of letters from girls and boys telling her how much they liked her books.